Special Thanks To:

My parents, my sister, as well as my mentors
Ronnie Sidney II, Jerome and Jeromyah Jones,
Sheryl Jones, and Dr. Anna Douglas

D1606693

Table of Contents

Character Catalog

Chapter 1: Meeting The Crew

Hi, my name is Arlo, and I'm a very weird kid. Wait, let me explain why, though. You see, I'm not your typical everyday teenager. Although, some of us are clearly different from one another. But I manage to stay my best self. Yea, I love video games and cars, but that's not all. Now, you're probably thinking, Arlo, you literally sound like a normal teenager but, no. I'm also a teenage detective. I love solving mysteries, no matter how crazy they are. I know, shocker, right? You didn't see that coming, did ya? My secret is that I have these amazing abilities to solve even the most ridiculous mysteries of all time. Well, at least that's what my best friend Rasco said. Rasco is my number one man. Even though he's a little.........wild. He was my first friend in fourth grade when my parents and I moved down here from Virginia. It's August, and you know what that means. Yep, a back to- school pool party with all my friends from Parlym Middle School.

Now, I know what you're thinking,.... Arlo, what the heck is a back-to-school pool party? That's a very good question, and I'll tell you. My friend, Kensey's aunt, hosts an event called the

Back- to- School Pool Party every year. She does it every year near the end of August. It's really fun. There are water slides, water balloon fights, a lazy river. Heck, there's even this inflatable maze where people can have water gun fights. It's like a battle royale game but with water guns. Then, once it's all over, we all get to go inside to do even more fun activities. But, mostly Rasco, Mitch and I just mess around. Last year Rasco put a spider in the girls' room. All the girls were freaking out. It was hilarious!

It was about ten in the morning when my mom busted into my room, asking if I was ready. "Did you get everything?" she asked. "Yep," I responded as we walked downstairs to the garage. My dad was on a business trip to Europe so, it was only my mom, my siblings, and me at the house. I only have two siblings, though; my older sister and my younger brother.

"The pool party sounds like a great idea for back to- school, doesn't it, Arlo?" My mom asked me. "More like the most brilliant idea in the universe!" I said with excitement. "okay, okay, Arlo, don't get too excited now." My mom said. Kensey's aunt lived in Miami, so it wasn't that far.

We were only on the road for twenty-five minutes or so. For me, it felt like twenty hours. I could feel my adrenaline pumping harder every second we got closer to Miami. Not to mention I was exhausted. Not only because I didn't get the chance to play my basketball and battle royale games but, the fact that this is my second to last week of summer. We soon got to her house and, let me tell you, I thought I pulled up into the White House because it was huge! Five garages, ten acres of land front and back, a pool, and a hot tub. The mailbox had balloons saying, **"Pool party over here!"** As we got closer to the driveway, Kensey was standing on the patio in her bikini and a stack of white note cards. She gave me a friendly greeting along with a hug when I got out of the car." Hey, Arlo I, missed you these past months," she said. "What do you mean? We saw each other at the Fourth of July cookout, remember?"

" Yea, but hey, it's always great to see you again," She said. "wanna come in? Rasco and Mitch are already here." "Awesome," I said. I walked through the hallway to the living room, where I saw Rasco on his phone, probably watching videos and memes and Mitch playing his steel drums as he does all the time when he's bored. "Yo, what up Arlo bout' time you showed up," Rasco said. In case you didn't know, this is Rasco, one of my best friends in school. He's from the Caribbean so, sometimes he speaks in Caribbean tongue. He's also daredevil! Ha, I remember when he ate one-hundred green spicy peppers for one-hundred dollars and didn't even drink milk. Now, that's a savage. "Hey, nice to see you guys again," I said.

"It's also good to see yuh (yuh means "you" in Trinidadian slang), my brother but umm.......why you look so obzokee (Ob suki)? " Rasco asked. "What?" I asked him. "What do you mean?" "I mean, why you look so crooked, man? Yuh look like someone gave yuh a real one to the back." Rasco explained, "Yea, where's your swimming trunks, dude?" Said Mitch. "why don't you have them on?" "It's in my bag," I stated, "besides, I'll put them on later. We're here for a week anyways." "I guess you're right, Arlo. I'm just waiting for this show to get on the road after all." Rasco said.

The doorbell ranged, and Kensey ran across the house to answer it. It was Megan and Elizabeth, but we call Megan- Queens because she's from New York. She can be very sassy sometimes and struts around like she owns the place. On the other hand, Elizabeth, which we call Liz because she hates being called by her first name. She's more like your creepy, goth, soulless girl, you know? She's cool and all during Halloween but, for other events, she doesn't really....you know, show it. "Heyy, girls." Said Kensey. "Heyy," They all giggled. Queens and Liz were both in their bikinis and met the rest of us in the living room. Thank goodness I saw them too.

Liz always tries to scare someone from coming out of nowhere seriously; she'll be in one room location and then somehow appear in another location. How does she do it? I think she is a real vampire. "What up, Queens," Mitch said, laid back. "Mitch, why aren't you in your swimming trunks?" Queens asked. "Well, I gotta play me steeldrums to keep that chill vibe going on, ya know?" He answered. None of us knew what in blazes he meant by that so, we all decided to change the subject. "Sooo, Arlo, how about you go get your swimming trucks on. We're getting ready to start the party." Suggested Kensey.

"Okay?" I said as I ran upstairs to the bathroom to change into my red and black swimming shorts. Then walked back downstairs.

Finally, about five minutes later. Mrs. Scott(Kensey's aunt) came into the living room. It was almost time for the splashdown to commence. I could feel it deep in my spirit, counting every second to the final countdown.

Chapter 2: Pool Party Splashdown

Everyone was screaming and freakin' out for the splashdown event to begin. Mrs. Scott then stepped in front of the slide doors. "EVERYONE QUIET!" Mrs. Scott yelled. Everyone got incredibly silent. "Thank you....., now, who's ready for some fun?!" Mrs. Scott chanted. "WE ARE!" We all screamed, but before we began, there's just one quick announcement I need to share for you all." Everyone tilted their heads back like our teachers assigned us summer packets. "Ughhh!" Everyone groaned. Oh, c'mon! The second when the backyard slide doors are supposed to open, we have to wait for an announcement?! The suspense is killing me. I mean, really! What even is this announcement anyways?! "You all will be given a white note card for knowing who your roommates are," Mrs. Scott informed us, "You'll be sharing a room with five people in each room.....besides that, that's all for now." My eye then started to twitch like a fly got caught in my eyelid. Did she really just make us waste three minutes to tell us we were sharing rooms with each other? Really?! Mrs. Scott then unlocked the slide doors and stepped aside.

Finally, now that that's out of the way, it was time for the party to begin. The sliding doors opened, revealing a pool park of heaven. "It's beautiful," Rasco cried as he swiped away a tear. "Woo-hoo!!!" Everyone screamed as we charged outside to the backyard. Mrs. Scott's backyard was like a water park. It didn't just have one boring little pool. It had multiple lazy rivers, a wave pool, and an inflatable maze where we have water gun fights. I'm telling you, it was like heaven's paradise, and I knew I was gonna go crazy.

I was in the lazy river on my donut float, relaxing while listening to the blasting music from the patio and Mitch's steel drums until Zack turned over my donut float and dumped me in the pool. "Ha, surprise, bro!" He laughed. "Thought you weren't going to get wet today, didn't ya?" "Well, I wasn't planning to," I said. This is Zack. He's like your very friendly helper at school. He helps everyone from math all the way to social skills. "Aww, man Arlo," Zack laughed," You're the only one who hasn't got soaked yet, dude." "Yea," I told him, "because I'm chillin'."

"Oh, c'mon, Arlo. Live a little," He said, "Besides, I'm not the only one who wants to chill all high and dry ." "Whatever", I said. Annoyed at this point, I exited the pool carefully to hang around the punch table. I grabbed a cup filled with Hawaiian fruit punch and leaned back against one of the house's outer walls. Just when I was about to finish my last sip of punch, a shriek filled the dark night sky. "Ekkk!" Screamed Queens, running out of the pool. "What's going on?" I asked. "Someone, someone.....someone peed in the pool!!" She screamed out of breath. I'm sorry, I'm trying not to laugh. Did she just say someone happened to pee in the pool? Are you pulling my leg right now, Queens? Quickly, I ran to where Queens was running away from. Finally, I made it to the scene where everyone was crowding around the pool. It was like there was a great white shark in the pool.

But I realized it wasn't that. The pool was turning colors from light crystal blue to dark, infectious greenish-blue. "Ewwww!" Screamed all the girls. Everyone started panicking until Mrs. Scott came rushing outside, wondering what the heck was going on. She blew a whistle to get our attention. "What happened here?" She asked. "Someone peed in the pool!" Shouted Brian. Brian is one of those nervous type snitch kids in class. He blames things on other people all the time and never takes responsibility. He can never hold water. "Ok, well, until we find out who did this." "The pool will remain closed." Mrs. Scott announced. "Boooo!" Boo'd all the boys.

We were all forced inside. Some of us had to even grab our towels because we were just wet. We dried off in the living room. Since there are only five bathrooms, a sign-in sheet with names that said who would need to shower in the morning or night. I, however, was on the night shift so, I took my shower, brushed my teeth, and got dressed for the night. I was sharing a room with Rasco, Mitch, and Zack. Rasco and I played video games all night while Mitch and Zack fell fast asleep. Kensey, however, is like the kid queen of the house because she has a room all to herself. Sometimes she even invites girls over for girl talks or something like that. Rasco and I were over at the TV playing pixel fighter 5G. "Man, what a day, huh?" I asked Rasco. "Yuh think?" Rasco responded, "Who do you think peed in the pool?" "Or should I say, who do you think was the **"party pooper"**, get it?" Rasco laughed. I looked at Rasco with a disappointed smirk and shook my head. Then, punched him in his shoulder. "Rasco, you are the definition of cringe, my friend," I said. "I know. That's why you got me." He replied with a smile. I gave Rasco a confident smirk as I put my arm around his shoulder. "Well, whoever it was, they're not just going to give themselves up like that," I stated. "You're right, heck, for all we know, it was probably someone who has a weak stomach and drunk way too much Hawaiian punch," I said. We both started to crack up laughing, just like old times back in elementary school. "Must be pretty embarrassing for the **"party pooper"** to be called out like that." Said Rasco. "Yeah but, who do you think it was?" I asked him. Rasco then responded in the most climatic tone. "Only one way to find out." "Yep," I said. "grab your trench coat and magnifying glass, Rasco. It's mystery time." Another mystery to solve and bet ya money we were on the case.

Chapter 3: Returning To The Scene

Rasco and I made a plan to get outside to the pool without getting caught. Since there were no windows in our room and we were on the second floor, we needed a plan to get downstairs without anyone seeing us. Although Rasco suggested this insane idea of tying up the bedsheets and, climb out through the hallway window. But then, I said.....nah. We could just sneak downstairs, through the kitchen, and then pass by Mrs. Scott's room and were home free. "Yep, we, fittin' to get caught," Rasco nervously admitted. "Oh, c'mon man, have some faith if we stay quiet, then we won't get caught," I whispered. The floorboards creaked and crackled as we tip-toed like we were in a haunted house. Finally, we got to the kitchen. Now we just needed to get past Mrs. Scott's room. This was going to be tougher than I thought.

Rasco and I got up against the wall. "Is she in there?" Asked Rasco. I pressed my ear against the door to hear if she was. Usually, you would hear the noise of a raging pig because she snores like there's no tomorrow. It was weird this time, though. Nothing, no noise was coming through the door. It was absolutely silent.........way too silent. Rasco and I looked at each other like we found the winning number for the lottery. Then, suddenly, we heard the front door open. It was Mrs. Scott and two men with hazmat suits on. You know, the ones that are bright yellow.

"Again, what are we doing?" Asked Rasco. "We're gonna get a sample of the water in the pool. That way, I can give it to Jack to run a D.N.A test on it at breakfast," I explained. "Are ya *bazodee* (*bazodee means "crazy" in Trinidadian slang*) man?! Ain't no way we're gonna do all that and not get caught." Rasco overreacted. The men then started walking in our direction so, I ducked and hid behind a bush and, Rasco hid in Mr. Snuggle's litter box. (Mrs. Scott's cat) Mr. Snuggles is nice and adorable to everyone except for Rasco. This is because one day, Rasco was caught eating cat food by Mr. Snuggles and Mrs. Scott, he claims it was by mistake cause' he thought it was cereal. If you ask me, it sounds like a whole lot of bologna.

The cat started to hiss and scratch at Rasco to death. I could tell the look on Rasco's face he was about to scream. That, and he was about to throw the cat across the hallway. "What's that noise?!" Shouted one of the hazmat men. They turned on their flashlights and started roaming down the hallway, looking for us. "What we gonna do now?" Rasco asked. "shhh," I whispered. "Follow me." Thanks to the spy movies I binge-watched over the summer, I knew exactly what to do.......RUN LIKE HECK!!!

Rasco and I took off down the hallway like we escaped Area 51. Mr. Snuggles started chasing Rasco; he picked up Mr. Snuggles and threw him at the hazmat men. Rasco had no other choice at this point. "YEET!!" Rasco yelled. "Ahhhhhh!" One of them screamed, "get it off, get it off!" We were a minute away from the backyard slide doors until we saw Mrs. Scott in the living room within eye contact at the door. "Crap," whispered Rasco, "How are we gonna get past her?" I thought about it and came up with a solution. I grabbed my phone from my pocket and called Mandy. Our only handy-girl at our school. She's always prepared to fix anything. Last year she fixed the principal's car with nothing but a bag of chips, a paper clip, and two electrical circuits. Pretty impressive, huh?

She came sliding down the stair handle with a piece of fishing string and a raw salmon. We set up the string as a tripwire with the salmon on the other side. After that, Mandy got the hazmat men to chase her and threw a bag of flour at them. When they tripped over the wire, they hit their heads on the floor, knocking them out, and Mr. Snuggles was distracted by the salmon. "Is that it?" She asked. "Pretty much, yea, thanks, Mandy," I said. "No probs' detective Arlo. I'll see you guys in the morning," She whispered. Hopefully, one day I'll tell her no one calls me *detective*........ but for me.

After we knocked out the hazmat men, we stuffed them in a closet. Mrs. Scott started to walk in our direction. So, we cut the fishing line and pushed Mr. Snuggles forward towards her as she got close. "Awww, what are you doing up this late, Mr. Snuggles?" She asked in a high pitched. "Mr. Snuggles ha, more like Mr. Salty!" Rasco teased him. Mrs. Scott picked up Mr. Snuggles and carried him back to his bed while Rasco and I jumped out of our hiding spots and sprinted to the backslide doors. Once we went outside, we heard nothing but the relaxing ocean breeze, seagulls, and..... pop music? We looked up at Kensey's bedroom window, where the pop music was coming from. "Why do girls have to be so loud ?" Rasco asked. "C'mon, Rasco, let's get this sample for Jack," I told him. I took a test tube and scoped up leftover water from the pool. "Got it," I whispered as I closed it with a cork.

"Cool, now let's get out of here before seagulls start thinking we're walking toilets!" Rasco explained. We soon stopped walking in our tracks when we saw a mysterious shadow figure outside Kensey's window. Keep this in mind Kensey's window is always covered by curtains and, every girl at the pool party was invited to her room that night. So, all that Rasco and I saw was just a shady, outlined figure with long hair through the curtains. The real question is. Who's the mysterious person?

Chapter 4: The Breakfast "Theory"

Morning came, and I was up at the crack of dawn, ready to bust this case wide open. I may be over-hyped due to the sugar rush last night, but I am as alert as a watchdog, ready to focus on the task at hand. When I finished my morning routine, I dashed downstairs and sat with Jack at the kitchen counter. "Let me guess," he groaned. "You got a case you want to crack and, you need my awesome hacking smarts to help you solve it?" "Yep..., you in?" I asked. "Well, since you're up bright and early, count me in, I guess," Jack admitted. I started discussing the case with Jack when Rasco came marching downstairs like he was in a parade.

"Heylo (Hey-low) everyone! "He yelled as he entered the kitchen. "What?" asked Queens. "Heylo,', it means hello, hi and, what's up cuz'!" Rasco explained. The whole room went silent as everyone was staring at Rasco. He then came strutting over and sat next to Perry, or school's smarty pants. You know, that kid who always gets straight A's in every class. I swear, he thinks he knows everything. He even reminds the teachers if they forgot to assign homework sometimes! Perry then turned around in his chair and looked at Rasco." But it's not in my dictionary," said Perry. "That's only because it's a rare language spoken by people who stand out," Rasco explained.

"Something, you nerds, should take some time learning about." "As if I would." Argued Perry, crossing his arms. "Yea," said Kensey."Plus, I think we all know you definitely stand out, Rasco." "Why thank you, Kensey I appreciate it." Said Rasco with an eccentric yet elegant tone as he took a bow. "What is this language even called?" Asked Mitch. "It's called *Gangety* (*Gang-get-tea*)," Rasco responded. "Woah, cool dude, can you teach me some words?" He replied. "Sure thing Mitch, old pal, here's an example for you. What does *consum' sin sum* (consume sin some) mean?" Rasco asked him, putting his arm across Mitch's shoulder. "I don't know?" Guessed Queens. "Nope," Rasco answered, "it means how are you?" "Ohhhhh," everyone said. "Is *Gangety* even a real language?" Jack asked. "It's more real than your social media followers, but besides that, yes, it's a real language to whoever believes in it." Rasco elaborated. "Technically, Gangety is a combination of real-world languages plus terms made by yours truly me." I knew Rasco talked in slang, but making up his own language was the next level of Rasco's logic. Jack and Rasco started arguing.

"Oh, back off, man!" Jack yelled angrily. "Awww, is little Jackie having a fit?" Rasco teased. "Rasco, cut it out!" Kensey demanded. "Aww, but I love it when Jack gets triggered," Rasco replied sarcastically. "Oh, shush, boy! The only thing you love is gettin' on people's nerves." "It's not my fault," Rasco answered, "It's one of my laws in Rasco's logic." "So, your logic is to bloody make me go off?" Jack asked. "Maybe...." Rasco said with a smirk. We all looked at him with confusing looks on our faces. It's hard to understand Rasco's logic because to the human brain, we don't fully understand Rasco in some situations. Some of the stuff he even does. Doesn't make any sense to me or anyone else. I mean, none! Rasco is basically another human species from another planet. He's probably smarter than us. "You really make no sense Rasco," Jack told him. "Yuh face makes no sense Jack. Quit acting like a baby!" Yelled Rasco.

Dear Kids,

I'm sorry I wasn't at breakfast this morning. I had an important business meeting. I won't be back until **Saturday.** So, I went shopping last night for food to last you guys for a week. **DO NOT!!** Open any exit doors or windows or IHOME will alert me.

Love,
Mrs. Scott

"Ohhhhhh!!" we all yelled. Sometimes you just have to scream "oh" for your friends when they go off on someone. "Anyways," I said. I gave Jack the test tube. "Who do you think did it?" I asked him. "I don't know?" he responded. "But, I'll tell you this, let me run a D.N.A test then, we'll see, yeah?" Jack explained. "Yessir!" I saluted. "Okay, at ease, soldier," Jack told me. There's only two things why I like the morning, Belgium waffles with maple syrup and watching Gamer Gods on my phone. Everyone huddled around the TV, probably calling dibs on the TV show we were gonna watch.

"I want to watch Black Queens!" Yelled Queens. "I want to watch a National Geographic on lions." Said Perry. "And I wanna watch funny animal voice-overs!" Rasco yelled. Then everyone got real quiet and stared at Rasco. "What?!" Rasco asked. "It's the only thing that keeps me entertained." "Hey, Arlo, can you help me with these dishes?" Kensey asked. "Sure, thing Ken, I answered. I picked up a sponge and started washing while Kensey dried them off. It wasn't long before I realized a pink slip of paper stuck on the cabinet above me. "Hey, look. You guys, it's a note from Mrs. Scott!" I shouted. Everyone came herding into the kitchen. "What does it say, dude?" Mitch asked. The note said this, *Dear kids, I'm sorry I wasn't at breakfast this morning. I had an important business meeting. I won't be back until* **Saturday.** *So, I went shopping last night for food to last you guys for a week.* **DO NOT!!** *Open any exit doors or windows or, IHOME will alert me. Love, Mrs. Scott.* Here's some background knowledge of what IHOME is? See, Mrs. Scott is Chief Commanding Officer at the Independent Security Agency who manufactures IHOME (*Independent Home Security Over Modern Environment*). Gosh, what has technology come to? First self-driving cars. Now self-security systems?! What's next? An escalating sidewalk?! The creepy thing is, it's actually an AI *(Artificial intelligence)* t that has eyes everywhere around the house. Well, not *exactly*. There are just cameras everywhere!

"We're trapped!" Rasco freaked out, "I ain't fittin' to die!" "We're doomed!" shouted a random kid in the background. Everyone started panicking. But I manage to stay calm. Everyone locked inside the house for a week will make finding the "**party pooper**" a lot easier. This case will be a walk in the park. I grabbed Rasco's arm and pulled him into the closet to talk to him. "I got a plan," I said.

"Umm, I also have a plan," Rasco said, holding his two fingers in the air, "and that is to get you a toothbrush and some toothpaste cause' yuh breath stinks more than Brian's socks." "Whatever, man. Do you remember last night we saw that strange shadow figure in Kensey's window." "Yea......why?" He asked. "Because I have an idea," I whispered with confidence. "Since we have a week to crack this case, we can interrogate all the girls that attended that party last night." "Then, we can ask them some questions about the incident. "First of all, gross!" Rasco said disgustedly. "Second of all, good thinkin' Arlo, bout' time, you use that noggin of yours for something."

We busted out the closet, yelling. This is a crime investigation! Everyone looked at us like we needed help (mentally). "Ugh, here we go again." Groaned Jack. "Okay, I need every girl who attended Kensey's sleepover party to please step up," Rasco shouted. About eighteen girls stepped up front. "Who's first?" Rasco asked me. "Daisy!" I announced, pointing to Daisy in the group of girls.

Chapter 5: Pulling Teeth
Suspect one was Daisy. Daisy was probably on my top ten suspects for the "**party pooper**". Although she looks innocent, she can sometimes

act real suspicious around other people. Last year she was the head of the candy smugglers. Last year, candy was banned from our school so, this secret organization was about giving out candy to everyone. Rasco even called them the candy gang and made a whole rap song about it. . Rasco, Daisy, and I walked into a room with a single light from the ceiling and a desk with chairs. We call it the investigation room. "Please, sit down," I told her.

I had a quick conversation with Rasco on how we were going to interrogate her. "Okay, we're going to do this like, good cop and bad cop. got it?" I whispered to Rasco. Rasco saluted, and we both looked at Daisy, ready to see if she had anything to do with the **party pooper**. "Greetings, Miss Daisy," I said to her. "Arlo, what's this all about?" She asked. "Nothing personal, Daisy, just business," stated Rasco. We all sat down at the table to start interrogating her. "Where were you last night?" I asked her. "At Kensey's sleepover party.....why?" she questioned. "Hey!" Rasco called out, "Doh, be asking no questions, just answer." "Geez, okay!" she jumped. In case you didn't know, "doh" means don't or do not in Trinidadian slang. "Can you tell me the exact location of where you

were standing in the room?" I asked. "I don't
know?!" she argued. "How am I supposed to know
that?" "I was probably near the window, I guess?"
I could tell Daisy felt super uncomfortable during
this. She started leaning in her chair with unease.
"Ah-ha!" I exclaimed, pointing my finger at Daisy,
"so it was you that spied on Rasco and me last
night. "What are you talking about?" She asked
with confusion. "The girl who peeked out the
window last night, was it you?" Rasco asked. "How
am I supposed to know?!" She yelled as she stood
up from her chair. "Hey, yuh better watch that
tone," Rasco yelled back. "Honestly, I don't know, I
swear." Daisy hollered. "Put it on yuh momma then."
Rasco dared her. "Look, guys", Daisy answered,
leaning back in her chair. "If you really wanna know
who did it so badly, my suggestion is to talk to
Queens; after all, she's always keeping a lookout."
Half of what Daisy was saying was right. Queens
does have eyes at the back of her head. She's
always keeping a lookout.. "Very well, Miss Daisy,
you may be dismissed, thank you for your time," I
said with pleasure. "Whatever, weirdo," She
responded, slamming the door behind her. Up next
was Queens. And believe me, she's a tough cookie
to handle. Instead of cracking an egg, we would be
cracking a rock. I'm talking in a figure of speech,

of course. "Who's next, chief?" Rasco asked. I looked at him with a side-eye. "Bring in Queens," I told him. When Queens walked in, I could already tell she was not ok with this. She had the angriest look on her face, like someone bought the shoes she wanted, and there were no more left in stock.

She gave me a death stare and sat down across the table with her arms crossed. "Why am I here?" She asked. "Just give us the truth," Rasco answered, "and this will all go down easy." "Is this all about what happened last night?" She asked demandingly. "Hey!" Rasco yelled. "I'm the only one who asks questions around here." "Uh, I get to ask questions when I want to ask questions," she snapped. "Well, Queens, do you know anything about the "pool incident"?" I asked. "Oh, please, why would I.......umm.....why would I know," She stuttered. "Spit it out, dang it!" shouted Rasco. "I mean, I know a person who knows who did it," she admitted, "But I can't say because of-" But Queens couldn't finish her sentence in time because out of nowhere. A siren went off, followed by a loudspeaker saying. EVERYONE REPORT TO THE KITCHEN IMMEDIATELY!!

Chapter 6: Suspicious Activity Reported

When dinner was over, Perry ran over to me and whispered in my ear. "Psst, Arlo, I don't know if you noticed but, I saw Brian and Claire over near the stairs talking about something. I think it has something to do about what happened last night." He said. "Oh, really now?" Rasco barged in. "Well, what did they say?" "I'm not sure, but I'll keep an eye out for you guys." Said Perry. Ughhh, anything but Claire! Where do I even begin?! Claire is basically your typical bratty mean girl; her dad is filthy rich and is our school board president. She's also the cheerleading squad leader and hates it when people get on last her nerves. She's like, miss perfect little daughter. I walked over towards them to ask them some questions; I know, I'm nosy. But when I got over there. Brian looked at me for a split second and just ran upstairs. "Ha, flareguard." (*flare guard is a gangety term for coward or simply calling someone a chicken*) Said Rasco. . "Oh my god!" Claire snapped. " Why would you scare off Brian like that?!" "Hey, calm yourself down, Claire; I just wanted to ask you two some questions," I said, "but apparently, Brian doesn't want to cooperate." "Oh, whatever." She exclaimed. Rasco then came over, wondering if I hand a lead on Claire. Not literally, but metaphorically. "Anything new?" He asked. "Ugh, not you too, Rasco," Claire said disgustedly. "Excuse you?" Rasco mumbled under his breath with sass. "Look", I said to Claire, "can you not be annoying and just answer my questions?!" "Well, since you want to be rude about it, I guess I won't answer your questions", she said, walking upstairs. I could tell the look on Rasco's face he wasn't okay with that. I could literally feel his alter ego jump out and go right after Claire. I swear those two have beef, and if you don't know what that means. Look it up in the teenage dictionary (don't actually. It's not a real thing).

"C'mon Rasco," I said, "She's just wasting our time." But it was odd that Claire didn't want to be questioned. Normally, she doesn't even care. It was almost like Claire was hiding something? Maybe she was the **"party pooper"**?But I wasn't one-hundred percent sure. At that moment, my phone got a notification. Jack texted me saying that he had the "theory" on who was the **"party pooper,"** and thank goodness too, as soon as I got it. I told

Rasco to get Mitch and meet us in the bedroom. When I got there, Jack had all his technology and science stuff out. "Jack?" I called out. "Yea, over here," he hollered. He had his lab coat on and looked like an actual scientist. "You said you had the "theory"?" I asked him. "Yea, I might," He replied. "I got the information you need." Jack showed me the data test on his paper. I really couldn't understand what it meant, but I did know, finding whoever did this was just the tip of the iceberg. We still had to deal with IHOME especially, if we have to work overtime.   "It appears that the test is analyzed to be someone with black, blue or green eyes, freckles and dark, light brown or black hair," Jack explained. "Annnd?" I asked with suspense. "Is that it, dude?" Mitch asked. "What do you mean?" Jack asked him. "You guys only gave me the sample of pool water. I still would need everyone's DNA to complete this.""Jack so, you're telling me we don't even know if it's a guy or girl. Do you know how many people in the house have black, blue or green eyes, freckles, dark, light brown or black hair? That's like half of the people in this house!" "Quit your worrying, Arlo," he told me, "besides there's only twenty-seven kids here. And there are only eighteen girls. Plus, It's not exactly done analyzing: besides, It's a really ambiguous answer, heck it might not even be true. Unless you three are willing to get feces for the DNA test." "What does this have to do with *Theseus*?" Rasco asked. "Not Theseus," I informed Rasco, "*feces*, you know, human waste.

Heck, some sweat or blood at least."
"Ohhhh......ew." Said Rasco disgusted. "Yea, I think
I will pass on that, dude," Mitch replied. "Will take
our chances on the test, thank you," I told him.
"Okay, suit yourself, "Jack replied, as Rasco,
Mitch, and
I left the
room and
went out
into the
hallway to
discuss
what we're
going to do
next.
However, I
had
thought at
the back
of my head
that Jack's
solution
was
probably
easier. I
mean, all
we had to

do was get feces samples from everyone with the following characteristics. It couldn't be that hard......right? "So, what now?" Rasco asked. I turned around and looked at him as I facepalmed my forehead. "Rasco, you know what we have to do, right? Rasco then looked at me with a questionable look. "Arlo, I know you're not thinking we are gonna dig down the toilet to get poop!" He overreacted. "Well, we could always clog the toilets," Mitch suggested. "Mitch, don't encourage him!" Rasco yelled. Just when I thought we had this case in the bag, It got harder real quick.

I took out a notebook paper and wrote down all the clues from Jack's data paper. Black blue or green eyes, freckles and, dark, light brown or black hair. Since we didn't know if it was a guy or girl, we wrote down everyone's name who fits that description and, it wasn't good, but it was a step in the right direction. We started with nineteen people and made our way down to six. Geez, who knew finding the party pooper was this complicated? I knew we should have done it how Jack suggested but, this is the fun way.

Chapter 7: Mystery Hot Spot

The six people who matched up with the description were Claire, Brian, Queens, Avery, Jack and, Mitch. But some of the people seem innocent already. Of course, it couldn't have been Mitch because he was playing his steeldrums the whole time, and it obviously couldn't have been Jack because he's helping us with the case in the first place. It would be dumb for him to frame himself. Unless, someone was framing him? "Cool, so, we're down to six peeps," said Rasco. "Yea, but look, Rasco, it's already Monday." "We only have till the end of the week!" I yelled. "Crap!" Rasco shouted. Then, an idea popped into my mind. I called it the mystery hot spot. It's when Rasco and I bring in the six suspects and hook them up to a lie detector. Where would we get the lie detector? Don't worry, I got that covered......kinda. "You thinking what I'm thinking?" I asked Rasco. "Oh yeah," Rasco said with excitement. We both scrambled downstairs, looking for the suspects like we were looking for a one-hundred-dollar bill. We did, however, were stopped dead in our tracks when Queens came stomping in our direction. Me and Rasco's eyes were as wide as a quarter, and our legs were shaking like a buffalo was charging straight towards us. "Arlo and Rasco!" We both looked at her, having no clue why she was yelling at us. "Do you mind explaining to me what the heck this is?!" She swung open one of the hallway closet doors like she had super strength. The same closet that we stuffed those hazmat men in. We were screwed.

My heart started pumping adrenaline through my veins like a Cherokee drum, and I could tell the look on Rasco's face he was about to take off running and leave me in the dust. He was about to until a whole army of girls huddled around us. Believe me, It was not what we were expecting. That's like every boy's nightmare, or maybe even a dream. Hey, I ain't judging. But, all the girls had evil looks on their faces. "Aww man, we dead man,

tell my wife I love her!" Rasco cried with fear.
"You're not even married!" I yelled while looking
confused. "Go ahead, tell us. Give us your
explanation for this?" One of the girls yelled. It's
obvious, Rasco and I was looking pretty suspicious
at that moment. We could tell them the truth, but
Rasco and I weren't no snitches. So, we kept our
mouths shut. "We won't hurt you, but we will if you
two won't start talking." said Queens as she and all
the other girls got into a fighting stance. They
began to move closer every second; we didn't say
anything. Rasco and I both looked at each other
and talked with our eyes.....it was time to make a
run for it. As soon as the first punch was thrown,
Rasco and I dodged it then took off running for
our lives. We weren't about to get beat up by girls.
Nah, ah, ah, not today, chief. "Get em' girls!"
Queens yelled. It turns out the girls weren't
playing today. One thing about an army of girls,
guys, is that if you're hiding something from them,
they will always, I repeat, **ALWAYS** one hundred
percent find out. Rasco and I weren't giving up,
though, until a hand came out of nowhere and
grabbed Rasco and I, pulling us into a room. Then,
there was silence, not even the smallest peep. We
both got blindfolded. "Arlo?!" Rasco panicked,
"Where are you?........ Wait....... hold on, is this one

of those smell detergent commercials?" He whispered, attempting to ease the tension with humor. Then our mouths were covered. "Ahhhhh!" We screamed. "Rasco-" I called. Unfortunately, I couldn't finish my sentence because of Rasco's constant screaming. I kept swinging my hand, trying to slap some sense into him, but someone had already beat me to it. After the sound of the slap, the room cut back into silence again. Our blindfolds were taken off in a pitch-black room. We couldn't see anything until a lamp came on and, let me tell you, it was not what I was expecting. It was Kensey dressed up in an all-black jumpsuit like she was a secret agent, along with the six suspects we were about to interrogate. Rasco and I were blown away. For some reason, the suspects looked like they were asleep. "What in blazes did you do to them?!" I asked. "I suppose you two knuckleheads were looking for these suspects, right?" She guessed. "Yea, and?" Rasco asked. "So, I offered them Hawaiian fruit punch with a sleeping pill in the drink." She finished. "YOU WHAT?!" Rasco reacted in a horrified tone. "Wait, how did you know?" I asked. She laughed. "Arlo, IHOME isn't the only one with eyes everywhere." When she said that, I immediately got an alert at the back of my brain that she sounded a little suspicious there. Was she really spying on us this whole time?! I took a quick look at the suspects. Yep, they were definitely knocked out. "What the heck Kensey, you had to do Mitch like that?!" Rasco grunted. "I would have brought them here while they were awake but, they wouldn't come peacefully, so, girl gotta do what a girl gotta do," she explained. We looked at her like she had lost her mind because, at this point, she pretty much already has. "What?" Rasco asked. "You won't get it. Only girls will understand," she replied. "Oh," Rasco said, "well, I don't get much of anything, anyways." I busted out laughing when he said that. Until Rasco kicked me in the shin. "Oww!" I screamed. "Holly hopping peppers! Why do you kick so hard?!" The suspects started to wake up so, Rasco, Kensey, and I took their blindfolds off. "Where am I?" said Avery. "Welcome to Canada," Rasco yelled. "What?" She asked. I elbowed Rasco in his stomach to let him know, stop playing around because this was actually serious. I know that Rasco isn't serious sometimes but, who am I to blame him. After all, it's Rasco. He's the funniest person I know "Hold up," said Rasco counting the six chairs the suspects were sitting in. "How come we only have two out of the six suspects?" For once, Rasco was right; where were Claire, Brian and, Jack? "Uhhhh, dudes?" Mitch responded, pointing to the wall. "I think I found where they went." We all looked at the wall where there was a broken air vent with three blindfolds left behind. "Oh, shoot," Kensey said, "By the way, have you guys seen Queens?" "Isn't she in-" But Mitch didn't finish his sentence because we randomly heard an aggressive knock at the door. "Arlo, Rasco, open up! I know y'all in there!!" Said a voice. Rasco and I jumped up. " Never mind, I think we've found her," Kensey said. "Everyone remained silent," she whispered. We then all hid behind Kensey. She stared at the door waiting for someone to enter. It slowly opened with Queens standing there in front of all the girls that were chasing us. "Well, well, well, well. Looks like we caught ourselves some runaways. Thinkin' they're slick to get away, huh?" Said Queens in a western accent.

Kensey and Queens both gave each other a death stare. "Hand over the boys and, I'll be on my way," Queens said. "You're gonna have to get through me first!" Kensey said. "Dang Arlo," Rasco whispered, "Who knew your girlfriend was so protective." "Shut up," I told him. They then started walking towards each other. Just when they were about to fight, IHOME drones came behind the door into the room. "No violence shall be tolerated in this area." One of the drones said. "Please, report to the kitchen for your next daily meal." The drones soon flew away and, Queens and all the other girls left too. "I'll deal with you two later so, watch your backs." She threatens us. We, however, kept the remaining suspects to interrogate them.

Finally, we could do some real detective work now. When Rasco and I were done interrogating, we ran into the hallway to update the theory. Since Claire, Brian and, Jack wasn't there, I'm starting to think it was one of them. Well, Claire or Brian because Jack was helping us with this case the whole time.....unless he's helping them......I got a bad feeling about this one, chief

"I think it's Avery", Kensey announced, coming out of the room. I looked at Kensey with an overly concerned look. But, of course, it couldn't have been Avery. Avery is like the nicest girl here. She's not only Zack's sister, but she has the brightest green eyes like a glow stick, glowing in the dark. At least, that's what it reminds me of. "C'mon guys," said Kensey, "I'm getting really hungry right now. "Same here, sis'," Rasco commented as we made our way to the kitchen. "I'm so hungry, I could eat a eight-ounce steak."

Now, out of all things that Rasco has said in the past, that could be debatable.

Chapter 8: Going Down In The Basement

After dinner, I did my regular nightly routine and went to bed. Then suddenly, I started hearing a noise coming from outside the bedroom. It sounded like a rat scavenging for food in the kitchen. Well, it wasn't really a rat. It was probably Rasco looking for a bag of chips. I got up from my bed to investigate it. It wasn't easy with IHOME watching 24/7. If only I knew a way to get past that flying piece of junk with eyes. Then it hit me. I snuck my way to Jack's room. He immediately woke up. "What the heck are you doing here, man!" He shouted. "Sorry, Jack," I whispered. It's an emergency." "What is it now?" He asked. "Is Rasco being loud again for absolutely no reason?" I moved in close to his face and stared. "Ummm, mind backing up a couple of feet, mate? You're all up in my grill, yea?" he insisted. "I think someone is in the kitchen," I whispered. "Well, no geez, Arlo. It's probably one of those IHOME drones. Probably malfunctioning or something," said Jack facing away from me. Then, the noise started getting louder, as a bunch of pots and pans fell to the

floor, making a big non-stopping banging noise. "You think it's still a malfunction?" I asked him. "Shut up, and let's go see what you're talking about." He said, jumping out of bed. Jack and I both jumped into action and snuck downstairs. Soon as we got there, we saw the most random thing in the world. There were chips and crumbs everywhere around the floor. There was also a trail of.........lemonade? There was just a puddle of what we thought was lemonade, but we didn't know for sure. One thing for sure, though, is that it smelled and, I mean, really, **really bad**. Jack almost threw up just by the smell. "What the heck?" He mumbled. "Ugh, that's just gross!" "Who knows, it might just be apple cider vinegar?" Jack whispered.

We took a closer look at what in blazes had happened to the kitchen. Turns out everything that was on top of the fridge, like snacks and condiments were also all over the floor. The most snacks we saw were chocolate fudge-filled donuts. "Someone was here," Jack whispered. We both froze like statues when we heard one of those IHOME security drones fly by. "Get down!"

whispered Jack. Jack and I could not afford to get caught by these things. These drones are advanced high-tech. This means if you get caught by these drones past twelve midnight, especially if you're downstairs, it will automatically call the authorities. One even passed the puddle and began scanning it. When it was finished, it went into the basement. Uh, oh.

"We gotta get that drone." Whispered Jack. "Okay, but how?" I asked him. He quickly grabbed an empty soup can and threw it in the living room to distract the other drones. That way, we could get into the basement. Jack and I rolled to the basement door. It creaked and crackled when we opened it, like one of those creepy door sounds in scary movies. Mrs. Scott's basement is really creepy, though. Last summer, Rasco found a creepy rag doll under the stairs with a needle in its hand. Rasco said the doll was possessed but, I don't think it was. He's always so paranoid about scary stuff. We got down to the basement, where it was pitch black. I couldn't see anything, neither could Jack.

"Hey, Jack, you have a flashlight?" I whispered. "No." He responded. "But, I do have a flashlight on my phone." "Well, no shack Jack.

That's what I meant!" I whispered angrily. He turned it on, and he and I both snuck throughout the basement. "Dang, this place gives me the creeps. It's creepier than that haunted house we went to for Halloween." Jack said. The floors started to squeak and crack as we walked on them. For me, I was scared I was gonna fall right through. That's when a gust of wind passes the side of my face as if someone ran right past me. Then, it was that drone that scanned the puddle. It plugged a flash drive into a computer, probably containing all of today's security data. "I think it's trying to transfer today's security data into that console." Whispered Jack. "Do you always have to think the obvious out loud?" I asked him.

I silently sneak up to the computer when the drone left; I smoothly grabbed the flash drive and headed back with Jack. When it came back, it scanned the computer, then started to panic. The drone started flashing red and yellow lights everywhere. "Red alert, red alert!" It shouted. "System has lost data, last seen August 27, 2019. Launching search party!" At that moment, Jack and I knew that we had screwed up. Then, out of who knows where five human-like animatronics came out of their charging stations. Jack and I stood there with our mouths wide open like we saw a famous actor. These human-like animatronics were scary-looking. The drone started speaking in some type of code. "6_9_14_20_8_5_2_15_25." The drone announced. Jack then recorded all of those numbers down on his notepad. Soon, the lights started to get dim then the strangest thing started to happen. We heard loud noises happening around us, like someone was hitting pure metal with a bat. When the lights came back on, it turns out I was right. There were all tons of pits and parts everywhere and an aluminum bat laying on the floor. Jack and I jumped when the squeaky door creaked open. It was Kensey, Queens, and Rasco, probably wondering what in blazes was all that noise. At the same time, trying to figure out why we were down in the basement. "What in blazes happened here?!" Rasco shouted. "If only you knew." stated Jack, getting up off the floor and brushing himself off, "Arlo told me something was scavenging in the kitchen so, we went down to investigate." "You know what this means, right?" Rasco asked. "What?" We all asked him. "We goin' to court, boys!" He yelled. Oh no, not this again. I started talking to Jack as we all made our way upstairs. Trying to think of a plan to get out of this. Jack and I both knew once Rasco said, "We goin' to court boys!" There was no way he was gonna let us slide.

Chapter 9: Guilty With A Cat's Tail

Rasco grabbed his black robe, white wig, and gavel. You know, that wooden hammer judges use. Looking like one of those Supreme Court judges. We all walked up to my room for a midnight trial. "Order!" He yelled as Kensey shoved her elbow hard in his chest. "Imma need you to knock it down a few notches, Rasco. We're not trying to wake up anyone else." Said Kensey. "Okay, geez!" Rasco argued. "Let the court trial begin." It was sorta weird having a trial early in the morning while everyone was sleeping.

Queens was first up to establish her case in the courtroom. But, don't worry; it wasn't really an *actual* courtroom. It was just our bedroom. "Your honor I, Megan Ashaunty Lancy, or "Queens" is here to announce that Arlo is the **"party pooper"**!" Everyone gasped while I had a shocked look on my face. I had been framed. "What, how?" I asked. "Because," she replied, "I have proof." She started to pull out her handbag and dropped it on the bed. "Evidence one, a video of you and Rasco snooping around the pool three nights ago." Said Queens. I took a closer look at it and, it appears that the phone's camera mode was on thermal red. "That's weird?" I said. "Your phone doesn't have that setting, Queens." "Oh, shocker Arlo, I still have more proof where that came from anyways," she said. I wanted to yell at Queen's face so bad until Rasco hit the court gavel to shut us up.   "Alright, everyone, settle down, settle down," Rasco announced. "Miss Queens, is there anything else you would like to tell us?" "Oh, yes, your honor," she continued. "Evidence two, you and

Jack whispering about something on video."
"Really?!" I shouted. "It wasn't even that
suspicious. We're just talking about the incident.
Maybe, if you chicken nuggets weren't wasting my
time, I could have gotten the one who actually did
it!" "Silence! Don't you interrupt me!" screamed
Queens. "I'm not done yet. Evidence three is you
and Rasco scaring off Brian.

Obviously, because you tried to frame him
for the crime." "Peeing in a pool is not a crime,
dummy," I said. "So, you admit it?" She asked,
coming closer to my face. I leaned back into my
chair without a care in the world. "Not gonna talk
back, ah?" She asked. Then I leaned back on four
legs of my chair and stood up. Queens knew how to
play her cards in court. But, I was about to change
the game. "Your honor," I called out. "I call guilty
with a cat's tail." Everyone was shocked, except
for Queens. Everyone knew what guilty with a cat's
tail was. It was guilty of fake proof. "Ok, order!"
Rasco demanded. "Thank you, Miss Lancy, for your
brief discussion. Now, Arlo, would you like to call
someone to the stand to testify you're guilty with
a cat's tail?" "Yes," I said. "I call Jack to the
stand!" Jack got up and marched towards Rasco

turning his back and facing me. "Jack, tell the people here tonight why Miss Lancy's proof is nothing but a false statement."

"Well, I would have to say that her evidence is just bloody confusing," Jack explained. "For starters, it's quite unintelligent." Queens looked at him as if he called her a fraud, which he did. "Go on," Rasco said intriguingly. "Your honor, for example, evidence one clearly doesn't make any sense because some American phones don't have a thermal red camera option. In fact, I don't think any phones have that option. Except, security cameras. Queen's phone is one of those specific phones that don't have thermal red." Jack told us. "What, that's not true!" Queens called out. "So, where did you get that footage from?" Kensey asked. I could tell the look on Queen's face; she was sweating and looked really guilty right now.

"I..uh...mmmm...I have to go use the restroom," she shouted very nervously, running out of the bedroom into Claire's room. "That was....intense to the membrane", Rasco stated. "Yeah, you think Claire has something to do with all of this?" Asked Jack. "I think so", I said. "Ight' then, yuh crazy kids, I'll see y'all tomorrow morning, deuces peeps!" shouted Rasco. Before

Rasco went to his bed, I stopped him dead in his tracks to talk to him. "You think we gonna solve this case?" I asked him. "Listen, chief, I know, it's pretty ridiculous to be solving this case, really. But let me tell you what my pops told me a long time ago", Rasco told me.

"He said, no matter what you wanna do or what you wanna be, you do it like it's your calling." I couldn't really understand what Rasco was talking about because he was mumbling some of it but, I knew what he was trying to say. That's when another enormous out this world idea popped straight into my head.

Chapter 10: Comparing The Clues
After days and days went by, Thursday
came, which means we only had two days to get this
all straight before Mrs. Scott returns. I woke up

with three cups of coffee, a honey bun, and a big bulletin board with all clues to the case of the

"party pooper". Here's what I got so far. In August, Kensey's aunt (Mrs. Scott) hosted a back-to-school pool party. That's when the incident happens, and the party was a bust. Mrs. Scott suddenly had to go to an important IHOME meeting and won't be back until Saturday. So a sample of the pool water was collected for a DNA test.

Jack analyzed the data but couldn't find the match due to us not having the feces data. Jack, however, did establish a "theory" statement on who might have done it. Whoever the party pooper was had light blue or green eyes, freckles and, dark, light brown hair. Nearly six people matched the description—specifically Claire, Brian, Queens, Avery, Jack, and Mitch. Rasco and I took every suspect for a lie detector test. Everyone participated except Claire, Jack, and Brian, who were very suspicious. Mitch and Avery were off the hook, but the rest of them weren't. Like, when Queens ran into Claire's room after the trial, or Claire standing up for Brian for a weird and suspicious reason. Or, even Daisy acting weird when

Rasco and I questioned her about the human-like shadow we saw out of Kensey's window. Then the last two clues of me hearing a ruckus from downstairs last night.

Jack and I investigated and found a huge mess in the kitchen, along with the IHOME security drones everywhere. Therefore, last night there was a mysterious figure moving around. The same night, one of those IHOME robots was destroyed by a bat in the basement and activated a search party by expressing a code that Jack recorded in his notepad.

There are so many clues to solve this case. The only thing missing was our answer. I put on my clothes while Rasco and Mitch decided to be lazy and sleep in. I went down to the living room, where the strangest thing happened. Claire and Queens

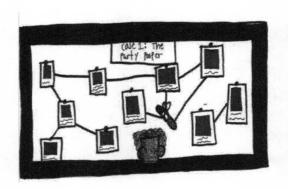

were on the couch in their pj's whispering to each other. I carefully stuck my head in the room to listen to their conversation. "I can't believe Arlo is trying to solve another mystery. I'm surprised they haven't solved this case yet," said Queens. "Don't get too comfortable, Queens. There are only two more days till Mrs. Scott comes back," said Claire, leaning back into the couch. "So what!" Yelled Queens. "It's not like they're gonna put two and two together." I started thinking in my head about what Queens meant by putting two and two together. Then, I started to get more intrigued and leaned in some more.

"Yeah," whispered Claire. "But you know how Arlo is. He never gives up. I mean, it's really obvious who did the "incident"." After those words came out of her mouth, I swiftly pulled out my tape recorder to record the conversation. I know, smooth move. "Shhh Claire, shushed Queens. "You don't know who could be hearing us." "Whatever," argued Claire. "Hey, I'm trying to help you!" Queens argued back. "And, don't you forget it. Remember you swore not to say anything about what happened that night!" Claire responded. They both started arguing like that for a while until this came out of Queen's mouth. "That's what Brian said, and yet, here we are. Keeping or mouths shut because of a fourteen-year-old boy who can't hold water!" I gasped, "So, it was Brian," I said to myself. At the same time, I was thinking about what Queens just said. But, hey, that's all the information I needed. "This is some bullcrap," Queens raised her voice. "Avery and Jack know about this, and they get to be off the hook." "It's just, I can't trust you," Claire explained. "Whatcha mean you can't trust me?!" Queens screamed. Claire stood there silently. "You know, you're just selfish, you know that! Caring about no one but yourself!" Claire then quickly pushed her off the couch. Queens then got up, and just when she could sock her in the face, I had to run into the living room before things started to get even more heated. "Hey, hey, hey! Break it up, you two!" I told them. Claire then gave Queens a smirk and mouthed out some words at her. "Say it to my face!" Queens yelled as she tried to go after Claire. Man, it was hard to hold back Queens. She was so strong. After the heat started to die down, Claire then left the living room. "I guess I'll call everyone down here." She said, going upstairs. I then let go of Queens, calming her down

"You ok?" I asked her. "Yea, thanks, Arlo." She said. I looked back at her with a disappointed look on my face. "What?" She asked. "I can't believe you," I said. "All this time, you knew what happened?! You just didn't want to snitch. Didn't you??" "You don't understand," She said, "I can't do anything. If I do, she'll...she'll." "She'll do what?" I demandingly asked her. "C'mon Arlo," She whispered, "Let's discuss this in my room as she grabbed my hand.

Chapter 11: Spillin' The Tea

We got to her room, and both sat on her bed. She looked at me dead in my eye and started spillin' the beans, spillin' the tea. You know, telling me all that juicy information I need. It's like what Rasco told me. If ya throw a rock in a field of eggs, one egg will eventually crack under pressure. "It was Brian," Queens admitted. I was shocked at the same time I felt stupid. But it also didn't make any sense; the shadow out of Kensey's window, Daisy's interrogation, the attack on the IHOME drones in the basement. All of that doesn't connect to this. "How?" I asked.

"It all started in the lazy lagoon where the slides were. Brian and Jack dared each other to see who would make it down the slide the fastest. Jack won, but Brian.....well, that was a whole different story. I mean, Brian did drink a lot of Hawaiian punch before the party. So, when he got down the slide, he splashed into the pool. Water went everywhere. And that's when he realized he **"party pooped"** the party." Queens told me. "I guess the splash was so huge, it was too much for him to handle. He tried hiding it, but it was too late. The pool started to turn dark blue. When someone realized it, it started a disaster, and the party got shut down." "So, what happened next?" I asked her. "Let me get to that." She responded. "Jack was there for everything and was going to say something until Little Miss Claire threatens him to stay silent or else. Jack kept his word. But not for long. He soon broke it when he told Zack about it, then Avery, and then you and Rasco decided that this needed to be solved. Who really was the "**party pooper**"?" "So, why did you run away?" I asked her. "Claire told me to not attract too much attention but, I guess that mission failed," Queens answered. Out of all things she said. That was the only thing that made sense to me. "Then who was the spy that spied on Rasco and I that night?" I said. "Let me guess, Claire?"

"No. Daisy!" Queens revealed. At that moment, my mind was blown. A plot twist so big, I was slightly confused. "She was nosey about the whole thing so, when she heard you and Rasco were on the case, she got even more intrigued," said Queens. "For example, when you guys called Mandy to help deal with the hazmat guys, she reported it to Daisy saying, Arlo and Rasco are going out to the pool. That's when she started staring out of Kensey's window, watching you guys collect.....something?" "It's not important," I replied. "Unfortunately, it was dumb and cost our cover to be blown. All because of you, Arlo!"

Queens yelled. "Hey, It's not my fault. You set yourself up. You're a rock in a hard place now," I stated. She then got up and grabbed a laptop from her desk. Which was weird because I don't remember Queens having one. Weird??? On the back, it said IHOME industries, and my mind went. Oh, okay, so, you stole this? "Where did you get this from?" I asked her. "Don't tell Kensey but, I stole it from Mrs. Scott's office downstairs." Said Queens. "WHAT!" I reacted. "Shhhh, Arlo, pipe down. Claire might hear you," She told me. "Does it look like I care," I told her, "At least I'm not stealing and lying under my best friend's nose!" "I had no choice", said Queens. "Listen, Queens", I said, "You always have a choice. It doesn't always mean it's a good choice, but it might only be the only one. So, why do you have this laptop?" "It's part of Claire's plan to help Brian escape. It's also where I got all that footage of you and Rasco," Queens explained. "Oh, you better spill about the plan, sister!" I overreacted. "The plan is for Jack to hack the IHOME system and shut it down. While Claire and Brian escape the house." said Queens. I couldn't lie. That was a good plan, but I was concerned because I didn't know when it was supposed to happen.

"Is that all?" I asked her. "Yea, pretty much. You can get out now", she told me. I got up and told Queens I was gonna solve this case. Then, I made my way to the door, where I saw the most ridiculous thing I have ever seen. Mitch, Rasco, Kensey and, Liz had their ears pressed up against Queen's wall. "We heard everything! She's a murderer!" Rasco overreacted. "What no," I said with disagreement. "Then what was it?" Liz asked. "This is crazy, dudes! There's no way Kensey's an actual murderer, right?" Mitch said worryingly. "No. No one even died!" I replied, shaking my head to the outlandish remarks. "Oh, really, huh? How do you know?" Rasco asked me, squinting his eyes.

At this point, Rasco had lost his mind. "Rasco, I was in the room," I said.

"That's not proof, my friend," Rasco said. "Just Shut it, Rasco. We heard everything out here." Said Liz. "Well, no duh, east-droppers!" I told them. "You guys literally had yall's ears against the wall." "I can't believe Jack was hiding something this whole time," Rasco complained. "That no-good absurd, musty, dusty-" Before Rasco could finish his sentence, lights started to flash, and sirens started to ring out. It was crazy, like a tornado warning. Then the IHOME drones, robots, and those creepy animatronics filled the hallways, repeating the same code that Jack recorded in his note pad. "What in the name of Hercules!" Rasco screamed. "Oh no," Liz whispered. "It's......It's a robot invasion." "We all gonna die!" Rasco shouted, while running down the hallway. Even though there was only one way to get downstairs.

We all started to follow Rasco, hoping he could lead us out of the IHOME mess upstairs. Fifteen minutes later, it turns out that mess was impossible to escape because we got caught quick. "Freeze human-like forms." The IHOME drone said. "You're not authorized to be in this specific area!" "Why not yuh bucket of bolts?!" Rasco chanted. "Rule number 75, no vile language in this household." "Oh yea, whatcha' gonna do about it?" said Rasco, daringly. "Is that a threat?" The drone demandingly asked him. "I don't know, is it?" Mitch asked. "Doesn't matter." The drone replied. "Please report to the living room immediately for a brief meeting about operation 6_9_14_4_20_8_5_2_15_25," It informed us.

The drone started pushing us to the living room. "Hey, watch it!" Rasco yelled at the drone. "My apologies, Rasco." The drone replied. We got to the living room, where surprisingly, all the other kids were surrounded by IHOME animatronics. The animatronics quickly departed from each other to let us in. They were blocking every exit you could imagine. "Scanning human-like forms for data." one of the drones said. I looked around cautiously to see if Brian and Claire were gonna make a run for it. But no, they're just standing there, like everything was fine. Then that's when it happened. All of a sudden, the drone started freaking out when it scanned Brian. "Target spotted," the animatronic ordered. Brian started to turn red and, just when he was going to say something, the scariest thing happened.

Chapter 12: Stuffed In A Cramped Closet

The animatronics started getting closer and closer, trying to grab us. Just when they were about to grab us, they randomly stopped and powered off. Then came back on with evil red eyes. "Welp, It's a wrap for us," Rasco whispered to me. Claire and Brian turned around, Claire having an evil smile on her face, "Get em'!" Claire told them. We all started to run away from IHOME before they could catch us, but it didn't last long. We got caught and stuffed in a closet. The exact same closet the hazmat men were in all this time. I was still wondering, where was Jack? Finally, there was a break of silence. It was darker than Mrs. Scott's black Mercedes-Benz. "Ugh, where's the light switch?" I cautiously asked myself. "Eww, Rasco, get your elbow out of my face!" Queens argued. "I would if your face wasn't next to my butt!" Rasco responded. "Rasco, I swear to blue poppin' peppermints if you fart, it's a wrap for all of us," Mitch said.

Then, there was a moment of silence. Before, it was disrupted by what sounded like an inflating balloon. But, a smell soon filled the air and, then, we all realized what happened. Rasco done dropped the bomb. It was like an explosion.

"Holy crap, Rasco," I said, pinching my nose. "What went up in you and died?"

"Ughh, what is that smell?" Avery asked in a disgusted tone. "Rasco farted!" I yelled. "Sweet primary chicken, what did you eat, man?" Asked Perry. "Let's see," Rasco suggested, "Uh....beans, chili, carrots and, an peanut butter jelly sandwich with a tuna sandwich." "I think I'm gonna throw up." Said Zack trying not to throw up. "That's disgusting!" Queens shouted. "Dudes, I just realized something." Said Mitch. "What?" We all asked. "If we're all in this closet, then what are Brian, Jack and, Claire doing?" "That's right, they're trying to get away!" Queens yelled. "How do you know this, Queens?" Kensey asked her. Before Queens could explain, I quickly interrupted the conversation. "There's no time for questions!" I interrupted. "We have to stop Brian and Claire from leaving the house!" I quickly made my way to the closet door, kicking it down with force like one of those SWAT officers you see on TV. "Arlo, wait!" Kensey shouted as Mitch and Rasco followed her while the rest of the crew stayed behind. I got to the living room, where I saw Jack, Brian, and Claire talking. "Freeze dirtbags!" I shouted.

Before, I could have gotten any closer to them. Instead, Jack pressed a big red button. And, I'm guessing he cut the power out because everything went pitch black. Then, Rasco ran straight into me. "Oww!" I yelled. "Bro, watch where you're goin'!" "My bad, bro." He apologized. Luckily, the lights came back on, thanks to Kensey finding the light switch. Along with Mitch exhausted from running up the hallway. "Dudes, why y'all dudes run so fast?" He said out of breath. He then fell to the floor, gasping for air. Don't worry; Mitch is just overreacting. "See, bro, this is why yuh gotta stop skipping leg day!" Rasco admitted. "Where did they go?" I said, looking for Claire and Brian. "What about Jack?" Asked Mitch. "Jack doesn't matter right now. We just need Claire and Brian." Said Kensey. Suddenly, I saw the garage door left open. "They went in here!" I called out. We all rushed into the garage. It was also pitch black in there. "Where could she go in here?" Rasco Asked. Before I could answer Rasco's question, I heard a sound like an electrical lion roar erupted in the garage. Then, it hit me. This was their plan. For Jack, to hack and shut down IHOME while Claire and Brian ride out of here in style. And, I mean, literally. Ride outta here with style. I slowly turned around and saw ocean blue headlights shine in my eyes. Claire must have broken into Mrs. Scott's key box and stole a car key to one of her sports cars. It was a crystal white Lamborghini Huracan. "Cya later loser squad!" She shouted. Flooring the gas and bursting out of the garage before I had time to move out the way. Is she crazy?!" Kensey yelled. "My aunt's gonna kill me if she noticed one of her sports cars is missing!" "What was your first clue?!" I asked her sarcastically. Before we could have argued like that for a while, we were interrupted by Rasco pulling up outside with a dark purple McLaren P1.

"Ayo, what are yuh guys waiting for? Get in!" He said. Mitch, Kensey, and I got in the car. "Rasco, you do know how to drive a car, right?" Kensey asked him. "I mean if it's in a videogame. How hard can it be?" He told us. He then hit a speed bump, making all of us hit our heads on the ceiling of the car. We all looked at Rasco with our eyes squinted to show how annoyed we were. "Whoops, sorry." He said. "Just try to keep us alive, please," Kensey told him. "No promises," Rasco responded with a smile. We got out of the neighborhood and, we drove into the city, where it was totally abandoned. There was destruction all over the road. Cars flipped over, tire marks everywhere. Even some buildings had broken glass. I told Rasco to go slow, like, ten miles per hour slow. When he did, both of us looked left and right to see if we could spot the car.

Chapter 13: Suspenseful Car Chase

A few minutes later, Rasco stopped to a complete halt. "What's wrong? Why'd you stop?" Kensey asked. "Look," he said. When all the smoke and dust cleared the air, we spotted the Lamborghini with Claire and Brian sitting there with despicable smiles on their faces. "Uhhh, guys. I think they're thinking to ram us?" Kensey guessed. The engine of the Lamborghini screeched and wailed as it got closer and closer to us. We all froze with fear. "Rasco, move the car!!" Mitch yelled at the top of his lungs.

Before Rasco could turn the wheel, Mitch snatched it last second and slammed on the pedal. "Ahhhhh!" We all screamed. However, I knew that wasn't the end. Somehow. Mitch pulled off a quick remover like a three-sixty drift, right before Brian and Claire could ram us. "Sweet lord of biscuits! What did Kensey say about trying to keep us alive?!" Yelled Rasco. "I just saved your guy's life. You're welcome, dudes!" Mitch yelled back.

Mitch was right. We ended up safe and sound on the other side of the street while Claire and Brian crashed into a mattress store. "Is everyone okay?!" Kensey shouted. "Yep!" We all shouted. "Ummm...Arlo? What is that?" Said Mitch, pointing to the rearview mirror. My heart started to race, and my eyes got wider than a tennis ball. I saw red and blue flashing lights getting closer towards us. And, they're a bunch of them too! "Oh, shoot, it's the cops!" Rasco shouted. "We gotta get out of here, gang!" "They're not really gonna arrest four teenagers, right?" Kensey asked. "I don't know?" I said. "But, I ain't sticking around to find out." Kensey then got a message from her aunt saying that she's getting off early and she's five minutes away from the house.

    "We gotta get back to the house!" Kensey shouted. "Step on it, Rasco, and make it snappy." "You got it, Kens'. Hold on to yuh seats!" Rasco hollered, slamming the pedal to the metal and driving us out of there. We have to get back to the house before Mrs. Scott did. It took forever but, we finally got there. Thanks to the operator, she wasn't there yet. We went into the house and saw that it was a mess. Sure, the hazmat men mysteriously disappeared, but there were all types of broken stuff everywhere. Like, broken animatronic pieces and plastic. "Heylo!" Rasco hollered. "Anyone home?" Avery, Perry, Queens, Zack and, Jack surprisingly came poking their heads into the living room. The funny thing is that Jack had his arms held behind his back by Zack and Queens. "Oh, you guys found Jack," I said, holding back my laughter. "Yea!" Said Queens, aggressively pushing Jack towards us. "He tried hiding in the basement after everything went south." "You're one to talk," Jack grunted. "I had everything under control!" "Oh, shut up, man. You're just salty because you got caught." Said Queens, "Yea, until that car chase happened, you could have gotten away." Rasco interrupted. Jack then looked very confused. "I think, what Rasco is trying to say, Jack is that you don' goofed up," I explained. Jack stood there silently with a straight look. "I did my job." He whispered under his breath. "Oh, shut up! You had no job!" Queens yelled, slapping Jack upside the back of his head. "Well, I best be on my way. My dad is picking me up, so I'll see all of you guys at school." Said Jack walking outside the door with Zack and Queens right behind him. "Bye guys," Avery shouted with delight, following Queens and Zack. "I'll also see you guys at school; y'all take care." Said Zack. They both exited the house and waited outside for their parents to pick them up.

       "Oh, yea," said Perry. "Kensey, I did the favor of calling everyone's parents to pick them up." "Yea, but Perry, how are we going to clean all of this mess up before my aunt gets back!" Kensey shouted with nervousness. "She'll flip if she finds out!" "Don't worry, Kensey, all we have to do is clean up all the broken IHOME pieces and will soon be Scott free," Perry stated. "Who's Scott?" Mitch asked. "Oh, goodness, it's a saying!" Perry overreacted. We all got to work. Sweeping, dusting, wiping, you name it. Then we heard a car pull up to the driveway. It was Mrs. Scott in her blue and white Mercedes-Benz. She walked straight to the front door. "She's here!" Rasco yelled from upstairs. Rasco, Mitch, Kensey and, I packed up our stuff and went downstairs to wait in the living room. Everyone else had already left early, so it was just the four of us. Mrs. Scott immediately burst open the door. "Kids!" She yelled, "thank goodness you're here. Where are the rest of the kids?" "They left," Rasco stated. The TV randomly turned on. "This is channel 75 news, coming to you

live from Miami, Florida. I'm Stan, the man."
"Mitch, are you sitting on the remote again?" I
asked. "Nope, not this time." He said. "Breaking
news this afternoon around 3 pm. Two sports cars
raced all around Miami. Unfortunately, police were
unaware of this due to the damage caused by these
cars. To be specific, a crystal white Lamborghini
Huracan and dark purple McLaren P1." We all
stood frozen with our eyes glued to the TV. "Police
did, however, find two teenagers at the crash site
of one of the cars. Names will not be said on TV,
but their parents face serious charges from the
state police." Then, Mrs. Scott's phone started to
get a lot of notifications, especially from IHOME,
which was bad. She also realized her white
Lamborghini was not in the garage. "Welp, that's
our cue," said Rasco jumping off the couch. Mrs.
Scott then turned around with a furious look on
her face. Holding her phone towards us, showing
that she was talking to Claire and Brian's parents.
She also showed us all the notifications she has
gotten over the past five minutes. "Oh, snap," I
said, trembling in fear. She then walked over to
the closet and saw all the IHOME robots and
drones were broken. "WHO IS RESPONSIBLE
FOR ALL OF THIS!!" She shouted at the top of
her lungs. We all looked at each other. At the same

time, trembling in fear. "Ah, man, she gonna kill us," Rasco whispered to me.

"You know what, since y'all don't want to admit who did it, I'm canceling next year's pool party," She announced. "I can't take this anymore, first, a wild spider, now my IHOME security?! Kensey, I'm going to have a serious talk with your parents." "Yes, auntie Anna," Kensey said, mumbling under her breath. "The rest of you wait outside. I've got a phone call to make." Mrs. Scott told us. I jumped off the couch and made my way to the door when Kensey grabbed my arm and pulled me back. She then hugged me and told me it was fun hanging out with me and everyone else.

"Whatever," I said. She then pushed me out the door, slamming it right behind me. "Bye, Arlo, see ya at school!" She hollered through the window. I stayed outside on the sidewalk for ten minutes till my mom showed up.

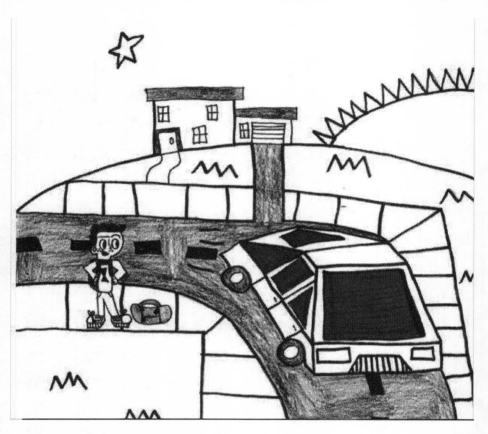

"Hey, Arlo," my mom said. "How did the party go?"
"It was...uh, it was-" "It was crazy, wasn't it?" My
big sister interrupted. "How do you know?" I asked
her. "I have my ways. That's all you need to know,"
she responded. "Oh, sweet lord of biscuits," I said
exhaustingly.

Chapter 14: A New Beginning

A month later, it was the first day of
school—finally, 7th grade. I woke up, brushed my
teeth, and shaved. Ha, naa, just kidding. I'm not
that old. But, I did eat breakfast then made a
break for the bus stop.

Rasco, Mitch, and Zack were already there. "What up, my brother from another mother," Rasco shouted. "Bro, it's too early for all of that," I said. "My comedy has no limit," Rasco responded with a smile.

"Rasco's logic also has no meaning to it either," Zack whispered to Mitch. "Dude, not, cool, bro," Mitch whispered, shaking his head. "Hmm...that's weird. Where's Claire and Brian?" Zack asked. "How am I supposed to know?" Said Rasco. "Last time I heard, they're tv famous." Finally, the bus came, and the doors swung open. One thing for sure, though, there weren't that many people on our bus, so it wasn't that loud. "Man, back to school. I can't wait to call all the nerds big heads." Rasco said excitedly. "Especially eating chili at lunch every Wednesday," Liz stated unexpectedly, scaring us, halfway to death appearing, out of nowhere.

"Are yuh trying to give me a heart attack?!" Rasco yelled. "No, just a surprise," Liz said with a settled smirk. "Oh, I'll give you a surprise, alright," said Rasco with a grin. "The sun ain't gonna be the only thing going down." "Alright, alright, you two, calm down. We didn't even start our first day of school yet." Said Zack. Then, we made it. We pass by a sign. Saying, "Parlym Middle School." "We made it, guys!" I yelled. Everyone started hollering and cheering as the bus dropped us off. Parlym Middle School is a little different compared to the schools in Orlando. For starters, our classes are inside, and our lockers and the 7th and 8th-grade cafeterias are outside. "Ah, 7th grade. We finally made it." Zack said with satisfaction. "All I smell is the ocean breeze and saltwater," Mitch said. I then left them as I saw Kensey wave to me.

"Arlo!" She yelled across the hallway. I then walked over to her. "So, you think we're gonna have any weird mysteries to solve throughout the school year?" She asked me. "Only time will tell Kensey. Besides, every day is a mystery in my book."

-"Everyone is talented in their own way. You should cherish your gift and share it with the world and young people."- Alfred Hill Jr.

THE END

Alfred Hill Jr.

Alfred Hill Jr. is a young author from Virginia. Born in January 2005, Alfred had a passion to write books and short stories ever since he was seven years old. He has a mom, dad and an annoying but loving older sister. You can follow Alfred on Instagram @ **Alfred_Hill709**

Made in the USA
Middletown, DE
11 December 2021

55177335R00050